TYPE·O·MATIC

To Mom and Dad, who read *everything* to me

ATHENEUM BOOKS FOR YOUNG READERS • An imprint of Simon & Schuster Children's Publishing Division • 1230 Avenue of the Americas, New York, New York 10020 • Copyright © 2020 by Lauren Stohler • All rights reserved, including the right of reproduction in whole or in part in any form. • ATHENEUM BOOKS FOR YOUNG READERS is a registered trademark of Simon & Schuster, Inc. • Atheneum logo is a trademark of Simon & Schuster, Inc. • For information about special discounts for bulk purchases, please contact Simon & Schuster Special Sales at 1-866-506-1949 or business@simonandschuster.com. • The Simon & Schuster Speakers Bureau can bring authors to your live event. For more information or to book an event, contact the Simon & Schuster Speakers Bureau at 1-866-248-3049 or visit our website at www.simonspeakers.com. • Book design by Sonia Chaghatzbanian and Karyn Lee • The text for this book was set in Courier New. • The illustrations for this book were digitally rendered. • Manufactured in China • 0520 SCP • First Edition • 10 9 8 7 6 5 4 3 2 1 • Library of Congress Cataloging-in-Publication Data • Names: Stohler, Lauren, author, illustrator. • Title: The best worst poet ever / Lauren Stohler. • Description: First edition. | New York : Atheneum Books for Young Readers, [2020] | Summary: "Cat and Pug are each determined to become the world's best poet, no matter what it takes. But can these two rivals discover the wonderful joy of writing together?"—Provided by publisher. • Identifiers: LCCN 2019020179 | ISBN 9781534446281 (hardcover) | ISBN 9781534446298 (eBook) • Subjects: | CYAC: Stories in rhyme. | Poetry—Fiction. | Cats—Fiction. | Dogs—Fiction. | Humorous stories. • Classification: LCC PZ8.3.S86843 Be 2020 | DDC [E]—dc23 • LC record available at https://lccn.loc.gov/2019020179

The ~~Best~~ WORST Poet Ever

Lauren Stohler

 Atheneum Books for Young Readers · New York   London   Toronto   Sydney   New Delhi

crunch
munch
crunch

A limerick involving
a fly and a flea?

A sonnet
to sundaes
with fudge
and whipped cream?

Whatever your style,
you ask and I'll do.
The special today
is a fresh-baked haiku!

Don't poke the haiku
this fresh toasty haiku, plump
with soft little words.

Seriously?

Don't be jealous.

You're probably at least
a little jealous.

Fine. Go ahead, then;
your turn.

I'm not jealous.

I could not possibly
be less jealous.

Fine.

They'll loop the moon!
They'll rocket back!

Scientists will start to track
a butt-shaped comet, shining bright:
a tighty-whitey
meteorite!

By tomorrow
Pug's Underoos
will dominate
the front-page news!

But who's to blame?
Who could foresee
this complete embarrassment?

Not me.

MEET the
METEOR 5¢

Something has happened,
much to my dismay:

The cat packed a bag,
and he went far away.

Maybe he got on
a pirate-y ship . . .

or maybe he took
an Antarctican trip!

Perhaps to a circus
to fly the trapezes . . .

or maybe to France
to eat fancy cheeses!

In any event,
he's not coming back,
so let's split his dinner—

And *don't open that.*

Here is a poem I wrote about pugs:
Pugs are as lovely as slimy worm hugs!

Pugs are like socks that are all full of holes!

Pugs are like oranges with too many seeds!

Pugs are like old boots without any laces!

Here is a poem I wrote about cats:
Cats are as fun as a tent full of gnats!

Cats are like soup, but without any bowls!

Cats are like gardens that only grow weeds!

Catsareasentencewithoutanyspaces!

If you were a pizza,
you'd be old sardines
with hairballs, anchovies,
and cold lima beans!

You're like an orchestra
filled with kazoos,
or a paper that prints
only yesterday's news!

Shall I compare thee
to a summer's day?
No, I shall not!
There just isn't a way!

Your autobiography's
title would be:
Somebody Farted!
No Wait, It Was Me.

If you were a sandwich, you'd be piled high
with licorice frosting and soggy french fries!

Well, *you'd* be a—

Wait.

Rewind, if you please.
Frosting, you say?
And what else would I be?

Limburger cheese!
Hot fudge that's gone cold!
Raisins so old,
they're all fuzzy with mold!

Magnifique! Do go on!
Please tell me there's more!
Is *this* what you think of me?
Mon dieu! Je t'adore!

How 'bout the old bones left over from stew?
Great greasy piles of mystery goo?
Dirty gum peeled off the sole of a shoe?
A big pile of something that smells just like—

WHOOOOOOOOOOO

OOOOOOOOOOOOOOOOOOOOOOOOOOOOOOO!

What delicious perfection! How tastily true!
You're a friend and a poet, and I never knew!
You've got me spot-on; now let me do you:
If you were a color, I think you'd be . . .

WAIT!

I can do better!
Let's try one more time!
If you were a . . .

Fruit!

You'd be apple pie!
If you were a . . .

Flower!

You'd be a bouquet!
If you were a . . .

Painting!

You'd be a Monet!

Oh my!

Oh yes!

Cat,
I'm quite impressed!
Of all poems ever,
this might be the best!

Stretch your fingers! Your brain!
We'll be at it all night!
To the typewriter, Pug—
we've got poems to write!

Now, how shall
we do this?

You first,
or me?

I'll pick the title!

I'll pick the theme!

What if we throw all these words in the air . . .

Let's try something different:
Let's go line by line!

I'll write the first . . .

and the second is mine!

If a line is too long . . .

. . . then we can enjamb it!

If a rhyme's almost rhyming...

it's not wrong; it's just slanted;

And if our line is a syllable over the limit?

Contract it! Just stick this thing in—

and we

'll skip it!

wi

See, we poets change rules
howsoever we like 'em!
It says so right here
on my poetic license.

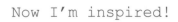
Now I'm inspired!

I've got genius to foist
on the poetry scene!

I feel poems brewing!

Cat, I think it's time
that we did our debuting!

Then anon and forthwith!

Yeah,
whatever *that* means.

Welcome to the World's GREATEST Poetry show!
world's BEST POETS